Nellie And The Dragon

All of a sudden, there was a roaring noise and a blast of hot air. Nellie and Meg, her dog, were thrown across the shed. Some old sacks heaved upwards and fell to the floor uncovering a large, scaly gold and orange body which had green legs and claw feet and a long green and orange tail. . . .

Nellie had no idea what to expect when she came across a dragon in the garden shed. But Gertrude the dragon soon let her know when she involved Nellie and Meg in plenty of adventures! The problem was, nobody would believe Nellie when she tried to explain that it wasn't *her* that made a mess in the kitchen or threw stones on the lawn but *Gertrude. Surely* they could see Gertrude for themselves?

Elizabeth Lindsay is the author of the HEGGERTY HAGGERTY series of picture books which are also published by Hippo Books.

Nellie and the Dragon

Elizabeth Lindsay

Hippo Books
Scholastic Publications Limited
London

Scholastic Publications Ltd.,
10 Earlham Street, London WC2H 9RX, U.K.

Scholastic Inc.,
730 Broadway, New York, NY 10003, U.S.A.

Scholastic Tab Publications Ltd.,
123 Newkirk Road, Richmond Hill,
Ontario, L4C 3G5, Canada

Ashton Scholastic Pty. Ltd.,
P O Box 579, Gosford, New South Wales,
Australia

Ashton Scholastic Ltd.,
165 Marua Road, Panmure, Auckland 6,
New Zealand

First published by Scholastic Publications Limited, UK, 1987

Text copyright © Elizabeth Lindsay, 1987
Illustrations copyright © Jim Hodgson, 1987

ISBN 0 590 70675 6

Phototypeset in Times Roman by
AKM Associates (UK) Ltd
Ajmal House, Hayes Road, Southall, London
Made and printed by
Cox and Wyman, Berks

Contents

For Beryl and John with love

1 Nellie Meets The Dragon

It was a cold, blustery, rainy day so Nellie had to stay indoors. She pressed her nose to the window and looked at the grey clouds scurrying across the sky. Meg, Nellie's dog, lay stretched out in front of the gas fire next to Sam, Granny May's black-and-white cat. They were both warm, very content and fast asleep.

The door opened and Granny May bustled in. Meg woke up at once. Sam rolled over and stretched.

"The man's here with the charcoal," Granny May said.

"What charcoal?" asked Nellie.

"That cheap charcoal your dad got. Fifty pence a sack."

"What does he want charcoal for?" asked Nellie.

"For barbeques," said Granny May. They both looked out of the window at the pouring rain.

"Some hope," said Nellie.

"Anyway," said Granny May. "It's going in the old coalshed out the back. You count the sacks, Nellie. And mind you count them properly. No dreaming. There's supposed to be twenty."

"O.K., Gran."

Nellie and Meg went to the kitchen, stepping across the newspapers that Granny May had put down to catch the soggy footprints. Boots came clumping down the hall and the man with the charcoal appeared. Nellie opened the back door, letting the wind in. Meg barked.

"Morning," said the man. "Friendly is she?" He had a sack under each arm.

"Yes," said Nellie. "Very. That's two sacks, Meg." Nellie shut the door before the wind got under the newspapers. When the man had put the sacks in the old coalshed, Nellie opened the door.

"I see you can count," said the man.

"Up to millions," said Nellie.

"That should keep you out of mischief, then." And the man tramped through the house for more sacks of charcoal. Nellie kept opening and shutting the door but she soon forgot to count. Instead, she began to dream of hot days out in the garden with chicken grilling on the barbeque especially for her and for Floyd, her best friend who lived next door. The daydream was so real that she could even smell the chicken. It made her feel quite hungry.

"That's the lot then," the man said. Nellie blinked and remembered she was supposed to be counting.

"Oh, right," she said.

"It was twenty," said the man. "What happened to you! Not very good for someone who can count up to millions."

Nellie narrowed her eyes but she didn't say anything. When the man had gone she ran out into the garden to check. There in the old coalshed were twenty sacks of charcoal piled one on top of the other. She ran back into the kitchen.

"What on earth are you doing?" said Granny May. "You'll catch your death out in that rain."

"It was twenty," said Nellie.

"Good," said Granny May. "Your dad

would've been cross if it had been any less. Twenty he paid for and twenty he wanted."

"Gran, we're going to have to have ever such a lot of barbeques to use up all that charcoal," said Nellie.

"That's what I said to your dad," said Granny May. "But if he thinks he's getting a bargain, he can't resist."

"If I put on my mac and wellies, please can I play in the garden?" asked Nellie.

Granny May looked out of the window. It had nearly stopped raining. "Go on then," she said. "Take Meg out and play ball." Meg heard her name and barked. Nellie rushed to get ready.

Everything in the garden was sopping wet. Nellie threw Meg's red ball and Meg disappeared amongst the Brussel sprouts to find it. Back she came with it, shaking it as she went. Nellie threw it again. It went even farther and disappeared in the cabbages. It wasn't lost for long. Meg soon sniffed it out and she came trotting back with it, wagging her tail like anything.

This time Nellie threw the ball really hard and it sailed over the vegetable patch and into the wilderness. The wilderness was the part of the garden that dad never got round to digging. It was overgrown with weeds and bushes and brambles. Meg loved playing there. She tore after the ball and scurried under the brambles. Nellie had to wait ages before she brought the ball back again.

"Good dog, clever dog," said Nellie. Meg's tail wagged furiously and she pranced, waiting for Nellie's next throw.

"This one's going over the rooftops," Nellie warned.

Nellie ran and threw the ball with all her might. It sailed over the vegetable patch, over the wilderness and landed somewhere at the very bottom of the garden. Meg dashed after it.

Ages and ages later Nellie was still waiting. She was fed up.

"I suppose I'll have to find it," she muttered and stomped down the garden path. She clambered over the brambles, watching for prickles, and found the ball hidden in a pile of leaves.

"Meg," she called. "Meg, where are you?"

At the very bottom corner of the garden there was an old shed. The paint had peeled off the woodwork and the window was covered in cobwebs. No one used it for anything now.

Nellie and Floyd had thought of using it for a den but never got round to it. Nellie listened. She heard snuffling sounds. She went to the door and found Meg sniffing and digging. Meg barked when she saw Nellie. It was obvious she had found something exciting.

"Meg, what is it? Is it in the shed?" Meg wagged her tail. The shed looked a bit creepy. Nellie turned the door handle and opened the door. Meg quivered with excitement.

The inside of the shed was gloomy. It smelt dry and musty but it was warm which surprised Nellie. There was nothing much in it. A flower pot, some bamboo canes and an old seed tray. In the far corner was a large pile of sacks. Meg sniffed her way cautiously towards them.

All of a sudden, there was a roaring noise and a blast of hot air. Nellie and Meg were thrown across the shed. They landed in a heap by the door. The sacks heaved upwards and fell to the floor uncovering a large, scaly, gold and orange body which had green legs and claw feet and a long, green and orange tail. Two sleepy eyes peered from the head on top of a long neck. The head had two large nostrils and two big ears.

"Excuse me," the creature said sleepily. "I sneezed."

Nellie and Meg were too stunned even to

move and sat wide-eyed. The creature stood up and looked at them. It began to brush itself down and flick its tail. It flapped its wings making a cloud of dust and yawned.

"I hope you're not going to sit there and stare," it said. "It's rude."

Nellie swallowed and pulled herself to her feet. Meg wagged her tail a little. Neither of them knew what to do.

"Don't worry, I'm not going to eat you," said the creature. It looked thoughtful.

"I suppose you know what I am?" it asked.

Nellie shook her head.

"Isn't it obvious?"

Nellie shook her head again.

"Oh, come on, can't you see? What's handsome and gold and breathes fire when it feels like it?"

"I don't know," said Nellie.

"Don't know. Don't know," said the creature, astonished. "A dragon, of course." The dragon bowed low.

Nellie gasped. A dragon.

"My name is Gertrude. Nice name, isn't it? Who are you?"

"I'm Nellie," said Nellie. "And this is Meg."

"I'm delighted to meet you," said Gertrude the dragon, holding out a dragon hand. Gingerly Nellie took hold of it and shook it.

"How do you do."

"Woof," said Meg.

Nellie and Meg watched as Gertrude shut the shed door and breathed deeply through her nose. Her hot breath made the shed nice and cosy. Nellie took off her mac and sat on a sack.

"How long have you been here?" she asked.

Gertrude thought.

"I've been asleep for about twenty years," she said. "I've been waiting for my wings to grow. They've come along nicely, haven't they?" Gertrude stretched her wings until they touched the roof. Nellie nodded. She could hardly imagine anyone being asleep for twenty years.

"It's nice to know there's still someone who believes in dragons," said Gertrude. "On the whole, people don't any more, you know."

"I do," said Nellie.

"I know you do, otherwise you wouldn't be

able to see me now. It's only believers who see us."

"I believe in lots of things," said Nellie. But I've never seen a dragon before."

Nellie thought how terrible it must be not to believe in dragons because then you would never ever see one. Her thoughts were interrupted by a terrific rumbling. Gertrude patted her tummy apologetically.

"Of course," said Nellie. "If you've been asleep for twenty years you're bound to be hungry. Can I get you something to eat?"

"Yes, please," nodded Gertrude gratefully. "Some coal if you've got it."

Nellie looked puzzled. So Gertrude explained that as dragons breathed fire, coal was the most delicious food in the whole world for her to eat.

"Well," said Nellie looking doubtful. "We haven't exactly got coal but we've got something that might do instead."

Nellie put on her mac, went and collected the wheelbarrow, and wheeled it to the old coal shed. With a great deal of huffing and puffing she heaved a sack of charcoal into the wheelbarrow and trundled it down the garden.

"I just hope that dad doesn't count the sacks. I'm sure he won't miss one."

"What is it?" asked Gertrude. She tore the

sack open with her claws.

"It's charcoal," said Nellie. "It's the best I can do. We don't have any proper coal."

"What do you use to keep warm then?" asked Gertrude.

"We've got gas fires," said Nellie.

"Gas fires. That's new," said Gertrude. "It was coal when I went to sleep." Gertrude took a piece of charcoal.

"Mmm," she said, crunching it up. "Not bad." And in no time at all she had eaten the whole sackful.

"Got any more?" she asked.

"Well" said Nellie. Another rumble came from Gertrude's tummy. "All right," said Nellie and trundled the wheelbarrow back to the old coalshed and fetched another sack of charcoal. Gertrude soon crunched that up too and wanted more. It wasn't until she had eaten three sackfuls that she was full up.

"Delicious," she declared, licking the charcoal dust from her claws with her long pink tongue. "Delicious."

Nellie turned to go. She could hear Granny May calling her.

"Will you be staying here?" she asked.

"I might be or I might not be," said Gertrude. "You'll have to wait and see."

Back indoors Meg settled herself next to Sam by the gas fire. Nellie went into the kitchen to talk to Granny May.

"Gran, do you know what? There's a dragon at the bottom of the garden," she said.

"Now don't start telling me all about fanciful daydreams just when I'm busy cooking," said Granny May. But Nellie didn't stop.

"She's called Gertrude and she's gold and green and likes eating . . ." Nellie nearly said charcoal, "likes eating lots of food. Gran, there's only seventeen sacks of charcoal."

"What!" said Granny May and in a cloud of flour she went out to the old coalshed. When she came back she said, "Oh, Nellie, you got the counting wrong. What am I going to say to your dad?"

"Couldn't we buy three more? Then he wouldn't know."

"Nellie, you're such a dreamer," said Granny May crossly. "I asked you to count them properly and you told me there were twenty." But she did go to the corner shop and ask Mr Patel if he had three sacks of charcoal. Luckily he did. He brought them round and put them in the old coalshed.

"Goodness me," said Mr Patel. "You've got enough. What do you want three more for?"

"It's quite a story," said Granny May. But she didn't tell it. When Mr Patel had gone Granny May said,

"Next thing you'll be telling me is that the dragon ate the other three sacks."

"But she did," said Nellie. "How did you know?"

"Get along with you," said Granny May. "What a grand imagination you have."

"Well, *I* believe in her even if *you* don't," said Nellie, stomping off in a huff. "And I bet Floyd does too!" Granny May smiled. Then she forgot about the dragon and carried on with making her cake. By bedtime Nellie had forgotten too. The next day was her birthday and she was so excited she could only think about her presents.

2 Nellie and the Flying Bicycle

Nellie was in the garden polishing the bell on her new bicycle. She rubbed until the bell gleamed. She dusted the saddle and the mudguards and blew on the spokes. The bicycle was very clean.

Floyd, Nellie's best friend from next door, popped his head over the wall.

"Cor, Nellie, is that it?" he asked.

"This is it. My best birthday present ever."

Floyd clambered over. "Can you ride it?" he asked.

"Of course I can," said Nellie. "I'll show you." And she cycled round and round the lawn. "Do you want a go?" she offered.

"Can I?"

Nellie handed the bicycle to Floyd. He took it gingerly. He held the handlebars and sat on the saddle. He'd never ridden a two-wheeler before.

"Now what do I do?" he asked.

"Put your feet on the pedals," said Nellie.

Floyd put one foot on a pedal and then the other foot on the other pedal and because he didn't move forward, ever so slowly toppled over.

"Why didn't you pedal?" asked Nellie. She pulled the bicycle off Floyd.

"You didn't tell me to!"

Nellie raised her eyes to the sky. "Don't you

know anything! You can't just sit on a two-wheeler. If you're not moving you have to keep one foot on the ground."

Floyd got up. "All right," he said. "I'll pedal."

He sat on the bicycle and put a foot on the pedal. He pushed down and as the bicycle began to move he put his other foot on the other pedal.

"I've done it!" he cried as he moved off. Unfortunately, the front wheel went over the end of dad's hose pipe and he did a terrific wobble which sent Floyd one way and the bicycle the other. They both landed in a heap. Nellie shook her head.

"I don't think cycling's your thing," she told Floyd. Floyd inspected his knee for blood.

"You might be right," he said.

"I'll tell you what," said Nellie. "I'll hold the back of the saddle and then if you wobble you won't fall off."

"Are you sure?" asked Floyd.

"Yes, really. It'll be fine."

Floyd sat on the bicycle for the third time and began to pedal. Nellie held the back of the saddle. It did seem to help. Floyd managed to go twice around the lawn before he did another big wobble and hit the wall.

"That was great," he said, pleased.

"I've got an idea," said Nellie. "You could fetch your go-kart and we could play dirt-track racing."

"Wow, yes!" Floyd shinned up the wall and disappeared over it.

"I'll have to wheel it through the house," he shouted from his garden. "It's too heavy to lift over."

"I'll go and open the front door," Nellie shouted back.

Floyd pedalled the go-kart through the kitchen and nearly ran into Granny May.

"Now what are you two up to?" she wanted to know.

"We're playing dirt-track racing," Nellie said.

"Make sure you mind the vegetable patch," Granny May warned. "Dad's just planted his seeds."

"We will," they replied.

Nellie and Floyd agreed that the dirt-track should go around the lawn, along the path, turning right behind the vegetable patch and back again.

"On your marks, get set, go!" Nellie shouted. They were off. They tore round the lawn with Nellie reaching the path first. Nellie pedalled along the path, leaving Floyd with a wheel stuck in the vegetable patch. He had just unstuck it when Nellie passed him on the way back. A few seconds later Nellie cried, "The winner!" She circled the lawn in a lap of victory.

Floyd completed the circuit looking hot and cross. "It's no fun getting stuck all the time," he complained. "Two wheels are easier than four."

"All right," said Nellie. "You take the bike. I'll go-kart this time."

"On your marks, get set, go!" shouted Floyd.

After a wobbly start he circled the lawn. Nellie was first down the path but came to a quick stop when a wheel slipped into the flower bed. Floyd cycled carefully by. Nellie pulled the go-kart free and pedalled after him.

They met head on at the end of the path because Floyd was on his way back. To avoid Nellie he steered to the left. To avoid Floyd, Nellie steered to the right which meant they both went the same way. There was a terrific crash as go-kart, bicycle, Nellie and Floyd landed in a tangle in the middle of dad's newly planted seeds.

They stood up rather shaken.

"Quick," said Nellie, seeing the damage they had done. "Quick." They dragged the go-kart and bicycle clear of the vegetable patch and brushed themselves down. They looked guiltily at the churned-up earth.

"You're dad's going to be really mad," said Floyd.

"You'd better take your go-kart home before he finds out," Nellie said.

When Floyd had gone Nellie sat glumly on the lawn. She didn't notice Gertrude the dragon come plodding through the brambles in the wilderness. Gertrude flicked her tongue at Nellie in a friendly sort of way. Nellie jumped up.

"Oh, it's you," she said. "I'm glad you haven't gone away."

"What's up?" Gertrude asked.

Nellie pointed to the churned-up seed beds. "We did it. Floyd and me. He's my friend from next door."

Gertrude swished her tail. "Oh, yes," she said.

"It was an accident but Dad's going to be really mad."

"Well, don't just sit there," said Gertrude. "Tidy it up. I'll help you."

It was too late. There was a bellow of rage from the kitchen. Gertrude scuttled for cover amongst the brambles as Dad stormed into the garden, his face bright red. "It was an accident," Nellie said. "I'm sorry."

"An *accident!*" he shouted. "You've ridden over the whole blooming lot. Where's that bicycle?"

As quick as a flash Gertrude shot from the brambles. She picked up the bicycle and flew into the air with it. Dad didn't see a thing.

"If you've hidden it, Nellie, that's it! There'll be no more cycling for you!'

"I haven't hidden it, honest."

"Well, where is it then?"

Nellie looked up. "On the roof!" she said.

Dad's jaw dropped open in surprise. Nellie's bicycle was wedged between the chimney pots. Gertrude was nowhere to be seen.

"How on earth did it get up there?" Dad gasped.

"*Well*," said Nellie. "There's this dragon. She lives in the old shed and she just flew off with it."

"Nellie, this is serious," said Dad, looking round for a ladder or a rope or something that would explain how the bicycle got to the roof. "This is no time for tall stories and make believe."

Nellie shrugged. She *wasn't* telling tall stories, she was telling the truth! She left Dad explaining to Granny May about the bicycle and went into the wilderness to find Gertrude. Nellie found her in the shed.

"No," said Gertrude. "I'm not getting it down for that old meany-boots."

"But when Dad's not cross any more, he'll let me have it back again," pleaded Nellie.

"The answer is no!"

Nellie could see that Gertrude was trying to help even if she was making things worse. But if she wouldn't get the bicycle down she wouldn't and that was that. Nellie left the shed and went back to the house.

"I've rung for the fire brigade," said Dad. "I haven't got a ladder tall enough to reach the roof. We can't leave it up there. If the wind blows hard it might fall down!"

Nellie ran to the wall and called over to Floyd. "My bike's on the roof."

"On the *roof!*"

"Yes. There's this dragon—she lives in the shed at the bottom of the garden. Me and Meg found her there. She put it on the roof."

"*Dragon*," said Floyd. "You don't expect me to believe that do you?"

"The fire brigade's coming to get it down."

"Wow!" said Floyd. "The fire brigade. Let's go."

Nellie and Floyd ran through the house and waited on the pavement for the fire engine. Soon they heard the siren coming closer and closer. It was exciting knowing the fire engine was coming to them. When the large red fire engine turned into their road they jumped up and down and cheered.

It came to a stop outside Nellie's front door. The firemen jumped out wearing yellow helmets and yellow waterproof clothes with big black boots.

"What's the problem then?" they asked.

"There isn't a fire," said Nellie.

"Thank you, Nellie," said Dad and explained about the bicycle being stuck on the roof.

The Chief Fireman grinned. "That's the best I've heard yet," he said. "What is it? A *flying* bicycle."

Nellie was about to explain about Gertrude and everything but didn't. "The firemen wouldn't believe me either," she thought.

The fire engine's big ladder was stretched up against the side of the house and a fireman climbed to the top of it.

"There's no bicycle up here," he shouted.

"But . . ." said Dad, turning red. "It *was* up there. It was wedged between the chimney pots!"

"Well, it ain't up here now, mate."

Everyone went through the house to the back garden to look. They could see the fireman by the chimney pots and he was right. The bicycle had gone.

"What's that then?" said the chief fireman pointing to the old coalshed door. Something was poking out. It was the bicycle. Gertrude was sitting on the wall. She winked at Nellie, jumped onto the grass and began to pick her teeth with her claws.

Nellie nudged Floyd. "There she is," she whispered.

"There who is?" asked Floyd, looking.

"The dragon, of course."

"Who do you think I am, Nellie? You can't fool me." Gertrude stuck out her long pink tongue and wiggled it under Floyd's nose. He didn't bat an eyelid. Neither did anyone else.

"Pooh, pooh, fiddlesticks," said Gertrude loudly. Nellie giggled. No-one else seemed to notice.

"What did I tell you," said Gertrude. "Non-believers every one. Even your friend Floyd." She strolled down the garden leaving Nellie wide-eyed.

"Well," said the Chief Fireman to Dad. "I *could* book you for wasting valuable fire brigade time but this time, I won't. How about getting your eyes tested, eh?" And he laughed.

Dad was speechless. He was beginning to wonder if his eyes hadn't deceived him. Except that both Granny May and Nellie had seen the bicycle on the roof as well as himself.

The firemen were very nice about things and, after a few more jokes about flying bicycles, flying elephants and that sort of thing, climbed into the fire engine. Nellie and Floyd waved as the fire engine drove down the road. Granny May took Dad into the kitchen and gave him a calming cup of tea. He wasn't cross any more, just confused.

Nellie looked at Gertrude sunbathing on the lawn.

"That means," said Nellie, "that I'm the only person who believes in dragons." She looked at Gertrude, who was tickling Meg's chin whilst Sam the cat was pouncing on her gently flicking tail. "I'm glad Meg and Sam do too. Animals have got good sense. It must be just the three of us in the whole world who can see her. I wonder if it is?"

3 Nellie and the Ice Cream Thief

One warm, sunny day, Nellie and Floyd were playing with Meg in the garden. Meg was holding one end of a rope, pulling and growling and being very fierce with it. Nellie and Floyd were pulling the other end.

"Nellie, pop to the corner shop and collect my newspaper, will you?" Granny May called from the back door. "There'll be enough money for an ice cream each."

"Are you coming to the shop, Meg?" Nellie asked.

Meg stood, her head on one side, the rope hanging from her teeth. "We're getting ice creams." Meg dropped the rope and trotted eagerly towards them. "Come on," said Nellie.

As they disappeared through the house a face peered out from between the brambles in the wilderness. A long pink tongue flicked round the face. It was Gertrude the dragon.

"Ice cream," Gertrude said. "It sounds delicious. Why haven't I had that before?"

Gertrude flapped her wings and sent the brambles flying. She flew onto the roof. In the street she saw Nellie, Floyd and Meg turn into the corner shop. Gertrude flew down and sneaked along the pavement. When she reached the shop she looked in through the shop window. She caught Nellie's eye and waved at her. Nellie came out at once.

"What's up, Gertrude?"

"Can I have an ice cream as well?"

"Of course you can't. Dragons don't eat ice cream," Nellie said.

"Why not?"

"It's *much* too cold. It would cool down your hot inside."

"Nonsense!" said Gertrude.

"Well, you *can't* have an ice cream and that's that."

"Huh!" said Gertrude and stomped off down the pavement.

Nellie and Floyd chose Choc Ices. Nellie

paid Mr Patel and tucked the newspaper under her arm. They set off down the street eating their Choc Ices. Nellie was so busy licking and

Meg so busy catching the melted bits that they didn't notice Gertrude on the lamp post. Floyd saw the lamp post but he didn't see Gertrude. He wouldn't — not believing in dragons.

They knocked at Nellie's front door and handed Granny May her newspaper. Then they knocked at Floyd's front door and Floyd's dad let them in. Gertrude stayed on the lamp post.

"No one cares about me," she sulked. "Not even enough to give me a tiny lick of a little old ice cream." And there she remained for ages.

In the kitchen, Floyd's dad was starting to make raspberry buns. Floyd and Nellie were going to help. They washed their hands, while Meg sat under the table and licked the Choc Ice papers clean.

Meanwhile, Gertrude was getting bored with sulking, especially as Nellie hadn't come to find her. Her claws were getting stiff and her neck ached because she'd held her nose in the air for so long.

"Well, there's no point in stopping here," she said and swooped onto the pavement outside the corner shop. She looked in the window. The shop was empty.

"I'll show that meany-boots Nellie what's what." She opened the door and slipped inside.

Gertrude tiptoed carefully past the counter where the newspapers and magazines were and looked along the shelves where the groceries were stored.

"Ice cream, ice cream," she muttered to herself as her eyes slid along the biscuit shelf, and the tinned vegetable shelf, and the lemonade shelf.

"Ice cream, ice cream, ICE cream. Of course, silly me, it'll be in the fridge. 'I' for 'Ice'."

Gertrude nipped round to the big refrigerator and started rummaging amongst the frozen peas. She tossed them hurriedly onto the floor along with the frozen beans, the frozen square fish in a packet, the frozen chocolate éclairs and the frozen roast beef. The refrigerator was empty.

"Botheroo!" she said. "Wrong fridge." She flung everything back all higgeldy-piggeldy and scurried to the refrigerator by the sweet shelf.

"Oooh! This is it," she crowed delightedly. "What shall I have? Everything," she decided.

Gertrude emptied a box of potato crisps onto the floor and filled it with ice creams. She

was about to leave when Mr Patel came in from the back of the shop. He looked at the scattered bags of crisps in dismay.

"What *has* been going on here?" he said.

He noticed the topsy-turvy mess in the

frozen-food refrigerator. "Goodness me!" he said. He saw the empty ice cream refrigerator. "We have had an ice cream thief. Oh, dear!"

Mr Patel didn't notice Gertrude who was standing with the crisp box balanced out of sight on her tail, her eyes shut tight and her claws crossed. He went straight to the telephone and rang the police.

Gertrude let out a sigh of relief.

"Phew," she said. "That was lucky." She pulled the wrapper from a Choc Ice and swallowed it in one gulp.

"Mmm, not bad." She dropped the paper on the floor and went out of the shop.

By the time she reached Nellie's front door, Gertrude had eaten *all* the Choc Ices, *all* the vanilla ices, *all* the raspberry ripple, vanilla, and peppermint blocks and only had six family-size blocks of chocolate ice cream left. She looked along the pavement and surveyed the trail of ice cream papers with satisfaction. She unwrapped the chocolate ice creams and scoffed them quickly. She put the wrappers in the crisp box and the box on the doorstep.

"That should cause some confusion," she said. "Serves Nellie right!"

There was an ominous gurgling from her tummy. Gertrude patted it gently. Something was making her feel a little uncomfortable.

"Never mind," she said and flew onto the roof, where her nostrils were met by the most delicious smell of baking cakes. "*Oooh*," she said. "I must find out where that's coming from."

She followed the smell into Floyd's garden and peeped in through the kitchen window. She was just in time to see Floyd's dad take the raspberry buns out of the oven. Very carefully, so as not to burn themselves, Nellie and Floyd lifted the buns from the baking tray and stood them on the cooling rack. Gertrude counted. There were twenty buns in all.

The front door bell rang and everyone left the kitchen, leaving the buns.

"Now's my chance," Gertrude said. But before she could move she began to tremble. Her tummy gurgled loudly and steam began to pour down her nostrils! Suddenly, she felt quite ill and the very idea of raspberry buns made her feel sick.

"On second thoughts, I think I'll go and lie down for a bit. I feel a little queasy." Gertrude staggered over the wall to the wilderness and the haven of her shed.

Out in the street, there was indeed a great deal of confusion. Granny May was on the doorstep of Nellie's house and Floyd's dad was on the doorstep of Floyd's house. Nellie, Floyd and Meg were on the pavement. Mr Patel was holding the crisp box in one hand and the ice cream papers in the other. A policeman stood beside him, notebook in hand.

"But who would *want* to eat so many ice creams?" asked Mr Patel. "They will be *very* ill."

"I should think so," agreed the policeman.

Floyd, Granny May and Floyd's dad were amazed at the number of wrappers Mr Patel had collected. Nellie knew at once who had eaten the ice creams.

"Nellie, I hope this has nothing to do with you," said Granny May.

"Or you, Floyd," said Floyd's dad.

"No, it wasn't us," said Nellie. "I bet it was Gertrude the dragon."

"Gertrude the *who?*" asked Mr Patel.

"Could you spell that?" said the policeman.

Granny May raised her eyes skywards.

"That's enough, Nellie! We don't want any of your fanciful imaginings at a time like this," she said.

"Only a greedy dragon could have eaten so many ice creams that quickly," said Nellie.

"Greedy dragon?" repeated the policeman. "It's no joking matter, young lady. There has been a serious theft."

"I'll tell you what it is," said Granny May.

"It's a complete mystery, that's what it is."

Nellie slipped indoors as Mr Patel and the policeman went back to the shop. She ran all the way to Gertrude's shed. The inside of the shed was freezing and full of steam. Gertrude lay tucked up under a pile of sacks with her eyes half closed.

"Oh, it's you," she said. "I feel terrible."

"It serves you right," said Nellie. "Fancy eating all the ice cream. I told you dragons shouldn't eat it at all."

Gertrude let out a long, miserable, steamy moan.

"You're really not very well, are you?" said Nellie. "I know what I'll do." And she ran out of the shed.

When she got to the kitchen she put on the kettle and fetched all the hot water bottles she could find. She filled them with hot water and carried them to the old garden shed.

"Here you are, Gertrude," Nellie said. "Put these on your tummy. It'll help to warm it up."

"Thank you." said Gertrude weakly. "You're a real friend, Nellie. I'll tell you one thing. I'll never touch another ice cream as long as I live."

"I'm glad to hear it," Nellie said.

Back indoors Nellie went to her money box and counted out what was in it.

"It's not a lot but it's better than nothing," she said and ran all the way to the corner shop. "This is for you to help towards the ice creams, Mr Patel," she said.

"Oh, Nellie," said Mr Patel. "This is very generous of you. But it is all right because my insurance policy will pay for the loss, I think. Don't you worry." And he gave Nellie her money back and a packet of chocolate biscuits.

"You go and share them with your dragon," he said.

"Oh," Nellie said. "Do you believe in dragons?"

Mr Patel smiled. "I'd like to," he said.

Nellie took the chocolate biscuits straight to the old garden shed. Gertrude's eyes lit up at the sight of them and by the time she and Nellie had finished the biscuits her tummy was feeling a lot better.

4 Nellie's Night-Time Adventure

It was the middle of the night. Nellie was tucked up in bed fast asleep with Meg lying across her legs, her nose buried in her paws. She, too, was asleep. The house was quiet. The only sound to be heard was the tick of the alarm clock in Dad's room. Nellie turned over and Meg fell off her legs. Neither of them stirred until Meg heard a tap at the window. She sat up wide awake and growled.

There was another tap. Meg growled more fiercely, her top lip curled, showing her teeth. At the third tap Meg jumped off the bed, stood on her hind legs at the window, and snapped her jaws. Nellie woke up.

"Whatever's the matter, Meg?" she said. "If you don't stop it you'll wake the whole house."

"Tap, tap, tap", went the sound at the window.

"What's that?" asked Nellie. She fumbled for the light switch and turned on the light. She got out of bed and crept sideways along the wall. She lifted the edge of the curtain. At first she couldn't see anything but black. The something pressed against the glass. Nellie yelped. She flew back to bed and buried herself under the bedclothes.

Meg sniffed at the window. "Tap, tap, tap" went whatever it was at the window, getting louder with each tap. Meg sniffed a familiar smell.

"It's Gertrude," she thought. And Gertrude it was. She was sitting in an uncomfortable position on the window ledge and beginning to get cross. She had gone to all this trouble to wake Nellie and what did she do? Take one look at her and throw herself back into bed!

"Some friend," muttered Gertrude. She gave up tap tapping and banged. "Nellie, wake up," she said. "Come and open the window at once."

Nellie uncovered her head with a sigh of relief.

"Phew," she said. "It's only Gertrude." Meg wagged her tail.

Nellie opened the window and Gertrude squeezed herself into the bedroom.

"At last and about time too," she said. She stood on Nellie's clown rug, brushing herself down. "What a wait."

"It is the middle of the night and I was fast asleep," said Nellie. "I thought you were a ghost."

"There's no such thing," said Gertrude firmly. "I thought we might go to the park."

"But it's the middle of the night," said Nellie. "It's locked."

"What is a locked gate to me?" said Gertrude. "I spread my wings and fly."

"That's all very well for you," said Nellie. "But I haven't got wings."

"No, but I could give you a ride," said Gertrude.

"Would you?"

"On this special occasion, yes," said Gertrude.

Nellie couldn't resist such an invitation. "All right," she said. "I'll come."

Meg wagged her tail. She wanted to go too.

"Will you give Meg a ride, as well?"

Gertrude sniffed. "Meg can squeeze through

the railings," she said. "I don't want to overdo it."

Nellie pulled on her clothes as quickly as she

could. She carefully opened the bedroom door. The house was still quiet except for the faint tick of Dad's alarm clock. Nellie switched on the landing light, and the three of them tiptoed downstairs. It was surprising how quiet Gertrude could be when she wanted to. They arrived downstairs with hardly a sound. Nellie opened the front door, switched off the light, and the three of them went out into the street. Nellie pulled the door to but didn't shut it — she wanted to be able to get in again.

The street was deserted. The street light lit the way. They walked quietly, listening to their footsteps echo around them. It was chilly and Nellie shivered.

"It's different going out at night," she whispered. "Kind of spooky."

Meg was enjoying her walk. She wasn't on the lead which meant she could sniff at all the inviting smells for as long as she liked. At the end of the road they turned left. This was the main road. Nellie had never seen it without cars going up and down before. There was not a car in sight. She shivered again.

"Night time is funny," she whispered.

"The only difference between night and day," said Gertrude, "is that at night it's dark and in the day it's light."

"I think I like the day best," said Nellie, beginning to wish she was still at home, tucked up in bed.

The street lights lit them all the way to the park gates. Nellie looked through the railings. "It looks awfully dark in there," she said.

"You're not afraid, are you?" asked Gertrude.

"No, of course not," said Nellie.

"Well, come on then, climb aboard."

Meg hopped through the railings and trotted off down the path. Gertrude turned her back towards Nellie. It suddenly looked rather small. But Nellie did as she was told and clasped her arms around Gertrude's neck.

"Do you *mind?*" said Gertrude, coughing.

"Sorry," said Nellie, loosening her grip.

"Ready?"

"Yes," said Nellie.

Gertrude flapped her wings and slowly lifted off the ground. They were as high as the top of the railings when a car drove past them. The driver blinked. He stopped the car and looked back. There was nothing there. He was certain he had seen a flying girl! He shook his head hard and drove on.

"The man in the car saw you," said Gertrude when they landed in the park.

"Didn't he see you?"

"No," said Gertrude. "I'm extra invisible at night time except to my friends. Let's go."

Nellie thought they should hurry in case the man came back to look for her. Gertrude took a deep breath. She opened her mouth and blew out a steady stream of flame. The pathway was aglow with flickering light. Gertrude breathed in and everything went dark. Nellie soon got used to it being light then dark and was able to keep walking in the moments of blackness.

"What a pity Floyd couldn't have come as well," said Nellie. "He'd have loved this."

The park looked quite different in the light of Gertrude's flickering breath. Nellie kept close to Gertrude's tail. She didn't want to get lost. Meg was some way ahead sniffing excitedly. In the moments of brightness Nellie could see her tail wagging busily from side to side.

"I know," said Nellie. "Let's do all the naughty things we can't do when the park keeper's here!"

"Such as?" said Gertrude.

"Walk on the grass in the flower garden," said Nellie.

"I already do."

"*You* do because the park keeper can't see you. *I* don't because he can see me," said Nellie.

"I've got an even better idea," said Gertrude. "Why don't we go rowing on the lake?"

"I'm not allowed in the boats unless either Granny May or Dad are with me — in case I fall in."

"Don't be silly," said Gertrude. "You won't be on your own. You'll have me to look after you."

"Oh, all right then."

Nellie called Meg, who came trotting up with her tail still wagging.

"We're going in a boat, Meg," said Nellie. Meg barked.

"*Shush!*" said Nellie and Gertrude together. Meg shushed.

Gertrude guided them to the pier where the boats were moored. She blew a long burst of flame. They decided to take the blue boat at the end. Nellie and Gertrude climbed in. Nellie reached out and lifted Meg aboard. She found the oars on the floor. Gertrude untied the rope from its ring and pushed them out into the lake.

"I've never been in a boat before," she chuckled. "This is fun."

Nellie took one oar and Gertrude the other. They began to row. The only problem was that Gertrude was facing the wrong way. The boat turned in a circle.

"If you're going to row that way," said Nellie, "you'll have to push, not pull."

"All right," said Gertrude. "I want to see where we're going."

They began again, this time with Nellie pulling her oar and Gertrude pushing hers. The boat began to move forward. Meg sat on the back seat and wondered where they were going.

"Let's row all the way to the island," said Nellie.

"Yes, let's," said Gertrude. She was just about to blow a large fiery breath when they heard voices coming from the other side of the park. They stopped rowing at once.

"Don't make a sound," said Gertrude in a low voice. "Not a single sound. Do you hear, Meg?"

Meg looked towards where the sounds were coming from. She wanted to bark very badly. A low grumble could be heard in her throat.

"I'll go and find out what's going on," whispered Gertrude. "You wait here."

Gertrude spread her wings and with a leap flew into the air. Nellie pulled in the oars and sat with Meg on the floor of the drifting boat. The voices were getting louder and louder. A light flashed between the trees.

"Whatever's going on?" wondered Nellie, wishing for the second time that she was at home in bed tucked up safe and warm.

Nellie peeped over the side of the boat. The light flashed across the water. She slid down next to Meg and held Meg's jaws together.

"Please, don't bark!" she whispered. Nellie could see the light above them.

"There's a boat adrift in the middle of the lake!" a voice shouted.

"Dratted kids," said another voice.

Nellie jumped.

"It's the park keeper," she whispered. "If he finds us we're done for. He'll tell Dad and Granny May and they'll never let us come to the park again."

Nellie looked into the sky, wishing Gertrude would come back. There was no sign of her.

"The boat's empty," said the first voice.

"I'll row out and fetch it," said the voice of the park keeper.

The light moved away. As soon as she was in darkness Nellie took out the oars, pushed them into the water and rowed as hard as she could for the shore.

The boat hit land much sooner than Nellie expected. With a feeling of relief she lifted Meg to the ground. She put the oars in the boat and pushed it out into the lake. Already she could hear the splashing of an approaching boat. A light shone across the lake. Nellie and Meg ducked down behind some bushes. There was more splashing. The light found the blue boat.

"There it is," said a voice. "Steady as you go. I'll just get hold of the rope."

They grabbed hold of the blue boat easily. Nellie and Meg heard the splashing fade away across the lake. When it was quiet again they began to walk.

"Find the gate," said Nellie.

Meg put her head on one side and looked at Nellie as if to say, "Don't be silly." Only Nellie didn't see her. It was too dark. She held tightly to Meg's collar so they didn't lose one another.

Soon they came to the water's edge. They turned round and walked the other way. Meg was puzzled. She wondered what Nellie was playing at. This time when Nellie reached the water's edge she splashed into the water.

"Oh, goodness," said Nellie realizing at last. "We're on the island." Meg had known it all along.

Nellie peered across the lake. The men were walking along the path. She could see the light. They were going and she was stuck. What could she do?

"It's no good staying here, Meg," she decided. "We're going to have to swim for it." She was about to wade into the water when there was a flapping of wings from above.

"Nellie," Gertrude called. "Where are you?"

"I'm on the island," said Nellie. "Over here."

There was a whoosh of fire as Gertrude guided herself in to land.

"Did you see the policeman and the park keeper?" she asked. "That car driver must have told them. They were looking for us. What fun!"

"I don't think it's much fun," said Nellie. "Meg and I could have been caught. We're stuck on the island and I've got wet feet."

"You're not stuck now. I've found you," said Gertrude. "Climb on my back and I'll take you home."

"And Meg?"

"I'll take you both, this once," said Gertrude.

Nellie held tightly to Meg with one hand and tightly to Gertrude's back with the other. With a great flapping of wings Gertrude rose into the air. She flew up above the park leaving its darkness beneath them and towards the street lights and home.

Nellie and Meg crept in through the front door.

"Goodnight," whispered Nellie.

"Goodnight, Nellie," said Gertrude, not bothering to whisper. "Great adventure, wasn't it?"

"Yes, I suppose it was," said Nellie.

She climbed the stairs and pulled off her clothes. She hung her wet socks over her chair and jumped into bed. Meg jumped up beside her and soon they were both fast asleep.

5 Nellie and the Paper Bag Band

One morning Nellie came into the kitchen and looked at the great pile of things on the kitchen table. There were forks and spoons; jam jars and coffee jars; string and two burnt wooden spoons; some old toffee tins and a dented saucepan. Granny May was on her knees in front of the kitchen cupboard.

"What are you doing?" Nellie asked.

"I'm having a clear out, that's what!" Granny May said. "I've been meaning to do it for months."

She got up and put a whole load of paper

bags on the table. "I can't think why I kept all those."

As Nellie looked an idea began to form in her head. "Gran. Could I borrow these things to play with? You can have them back later."

"I don't want them back," Granny May said. "It's junk. All of it!"

"Thanks," Nellie said and ran into the garden, Meg following at her heels.

Nellie climbed the wall and looked into Floyd's garden. There was no one there.

"Floyd!" she called, in her loudest voice.

"He's just coming, Nellie," Floyd's dad said from the kitchen. "He's putting his trainers on."

Nellie jumped off the wall and opened the

outhouse door. She dragged the garden table onto the paving stones and rushed back into the kitchen. Meg flopped down and waited.

Back came Nellie with Granny May's shopping basket full of jam jars. She lined them up on the table. She fetched the coffee jars and the forks and spoons.

Floyd came over the wall. "What are you doing?" he asked.

"We're going to be a band," Nellie said proudly.

"A band!"

"Yes, and it's going to be called 'The Paper Bag Band'."

"You can't make a band out of paper bags, Nellie, that's daft."

"It won't just be paper bags. Come on, help me bring out the instruments."

Floyd carried the old toffee tins and the dented saucepan outside. Nellie told him to fill up the watering can with water from the outdoor tap, which he did. He watched as Nellie tied the biscuit tins to the table so that they dangled down.

"If you fill the jars with water and put different amounts in each jar," Nellie said, "we'll have lots of different notes."

Floyd filled the jars carefully. In some he put hardly any water and in others a lot, but he didn't put the same amount in any two. Nellie took a spoon and tapped a jar filled with a lot of water.

"Tong," went the jar. She tapped a jar with hardly any water in it.

"Ting," went the jar. It had a much higher note.

"Lots of water for low notes and a little water for high notes."

"That's very good, Nellie," Floyd said. He was impressed. He took a fork and tapped his way up and down the jars. No two notes sounded the same.

Nellie had everything organized. The wooden spoons were to be the drum sticks; the biscuit tins the drums. The saucepan was to be the paper bag basher. Now they had to blow up the paper bags and stick up the ends with sticky tape. Floyd began blowing while Nellie went indoors to find the tape.

"Puff, puff, puff," he went and blew up a bag. It stayed blown up even though he wasn't holding the end tightly at all.

"It's easy," he said, when Nellie came back with the tape.

Nellie fastened the end of the first bag while Floyd blew up another one. Soon they had six bags on the table.

"Enough for our first tune," Nellie said. But

before they could begin a sudden gust of wind blew across the table and carried the blown-up bags all over the garden.

They rushed to collect them. Meg joined in the fun and jumped on one. "Bang," went the paper bag. Meg jumped back in surprise.

"Hooray, they work!" Nellie cried.

Nellie and Floyd lined up the five paper bags that were left and stuck the ends to the table with sticky tape so that the same thing wouldn't happen again. Nellie picked up the paper bag basher and a drumstick. Floyd picked up a glass jar tinger and a drumstick and they were ready.

"One, two, three, four!" Nellie shouted and they were off.

"*Bang bong ting ting tong ting thud pop, ting tong bong bong bong bong crash pop!*" Meg joined in as well and sang with her best howls. It was quite a din.

Granny May came out, took one look, raised her eyebrows, opened her mouth as if to say something and went back in again. At last they stopped.

"That was great," Floyd said.

"Yes, we're a really good band," Nellie said, pleased. "Let's blow up some more paper bags and you can bash them this time."

They began to blow up the bags unaware that a pair of narrowed eyes was peering at them from the wilderness. Meg's nostrils twitched as a familiar smell drifted towards her.

"One, two, three, four," Floyd shouted.

"*Bang, bong, ting, ting, tong, ting, thud, pop, ting, tong, bong, bong, bong, bong, crash, pop!*" And on it went with Meg in full voice as the chorus.

The eyes in the wilderness screwed up tight and large claw hands pressed over trembling ears as Gertrude the dragon tried not to listen.

"What a horrible noise!" she gasped. "There ought to be a law against it. Dragons are *sensitive* creatures. Stop it. Stop it at once!" she shouted.

It was no use. Nellie couldn't hear a thing, there was such a din.

"I'll show them. I'll show them," Gertrude said and disappeared into the wilderness.

The next six paper bags were lined up and

Nellie shouted, "One, two, three, four," when the first missile arrived. The band was too busy to notice. It landed with a thud on the grass, a great clump of weeds. The weeds were followed by a punctured rubber ball full of water and half an old car tyre. The band played on.

Gertrude went into the street and raided a builder's skip. Missiles rained down thick and fast. An old boot, a broken umbrella, a cushion and an old spring. Still the band played on.

Gertrude, getting desperate, flew above the lawn and dropped an old mattress. It descended like a giant bird falling out of the sky. The band stopped playing.

"At last," Gertrude screamed. "And about time too!" She flew onto the roof in a huff.

Nellie and Floyd could hardly believe their eyes. Meg approached the mattress with caution, sniffing as she went.

"Where's it all come from, Nellie?" Floyd asked, amazed. Nellie looked up and saw Gertrude on the roof. Her tail was flicking this way and that. Nellie knew she was cross.

"Oh, dear," Nellie said. "That's the end of the paper bag band for today, Floyd. Granny May's going to go mad when she sees this lot."

Nellie was quite right. Granny May *was* furious!

"How on earth did you manage it?" she asked.

"We didn't. It was the dragon. She got cross and dropped it," said Nellie.

"That's enough, Nellie. I don't want to hear any stories."

Up on the roof, Gertrude smirked and poked out her tongue at Nellie.

"I want all this rubbish cleared up and thrown away before dinner time," said Granny May.

Gertrude watched as Nellie and Floyd put all the rubbish in a big pile on the mattress in the middle of the lawn. It was hard work as there was quite a lot of it. When they had finished they stood wondering how they were going to get rid of it.

"I could get the wheelbarrow. We could wheel it through the house bit by bit, and put it in the builder's skip," said Floyd.

"That's where most of it comes from," said Nellie. "I remember seeing that broken umbrella."

Floyd looked at Nellie. She didn't look as if she was fibbing.

"Well, anyway," he said. "We'll never manage the mattress. How the wind blew that over I'll never know."

"It wasn't the wind, Floyd," said Nellie.

"All right. I know. I know. It was the dragon," said Floyd.

"Yes, it was," said Nellie getting cross and turning pink. She pushed Floyd across the grass. "Why don't you *ever* believe me?"

"Well," said Floyd. "Dragons!" And he shrugged his shoulders.

Gertrude, smelling trouble, relented. She waited until Floyd was looking straight at the mattress. She swooped down, picked it up and flew off with it over the house to the builder's skip.

Floyd couldn't believe his eyes.

"Cor, did you see that?" he said. "The wind did it again. It just lifted it up. I've read about things like that but I've never seen it before."

"There is no wind," said Nellie. "It was the dragon."

"It was a freak wind, then," said Floyd. "You know I don't believe all that stuff about dragons."

It was Nellie's turn to shrug. She waved at Gertrude who was balancing with one foot on a chimney pot and said, "Come on. Let's go and see if there are any biscuits in the tin."

Floyd screwed up his face. He didn't really know what to think. He hadn't seen a dragon, just the mattress go up in the air. If there was a dragon how come Nellie could see it and he couldn't? He shook his head and followed Nellie and Meg indoors.

6 Nellie and the Midnight Burglar

Nellie was tucked up in bed fast asleep. Meg was curled up on her feet and Sam was asleep next to her with his head on the pillow. Everyone in the house was lost in dreams.

From the shed at the bottom of the garden came a rustle and a bump. The door of the shed opened and Gertrude sniffed the chilly night air. She came outside.

"I'm hungry," she sighed. She stretched her wings, wriggled her tail and felt empty in her middle. She scrambled through the brambles and plodded round the vegetable patch. She looked up at Nellie's window.

"Fast asleep, I bet," she said. "And me starving. I'll have to see what I can find." She tiptoed across the grass to the paving stones and tried the old coal-shed door. It was bolted and try as she might Gertrude couldn't move the bolt.

"Charcoal's off," she said. She tried the back door handle. The door was locked. "Botheroo."

Gertrude went to the window. It was open a tiny bit at the bottom. She wriggled her claws in through the crack and pushed. The window slid up without a sound. It was easy.

"Tee hee," she whispered. "I'm in." She heaved herself onto the window sill and with a bit of squeezing and puffing and pushing landed on the kitchen floor.

Meg awoke in an instant and was about to

bark when her nose told her it was only Gertrude. She wondered what Gertrude was doing indoors and fell asleep again.

Gertrude switched on the kitchen light and looked about her. The refrigerator was the first place she raided. Inside it she found cheese, tomatoes, a lettuce, some radishes, a cucumber, a cabbage, some cream doughnuts and some milk. It was a feast! Gertrude munched and crunched and drank everything, paper and bottles as well.

"Delicious," she burped when the refrigerator was empty. "What's for seconds?"

In the middle of the table was the biscuit tin and it was full because Dad had been shopping the day before. Nellie was not allowed to eat many biscuits because Granny May said they were bad for your teeth and made you fat. But Gertrude didn't know this. If she had she wouldn't have cared! She ate a packet of chocolate digestives in one go. Then a packet of custard creams followed by a packet of rich tea biscuits. She thought the fig rolls particularly nice, especially the crinkly papers, and quite liked the butter osbornes. She loved the Garibaldi biscuits but thought the plain digestives boring. The biscuit tin was empty.

"I need thirds," Gertrude said. "*Very* badly." She turned to the kitchen cupboard.

She found the cupboard disappointing. She ate a bag of almonds, finished off a packet of currants and wondered what to do with the bag of flour. It seemed a bit dry to eat on its own.

But then she had a brilliant idea. She would make pancakes! Nellie had told her how good pancakes were. It didn't matter that she had drunk all the milk. She would use water instead.

In another cupboard Gertrude found a big mixing bowl. She tossed the whole bag of flour

into the bowl, paper and all, and poured in some water. She stirred the mixture with a wooden spoon until it was nice and sticky and the paper bag was in bits. Then she poured the pancake mixture into the frying pan and fiddled with the knobs on the cooker. Nothing happened.

"Oh, botheroo," she said and decided to cook the pancake herself.

Gertrude held the frying pan out of the window and took a deep breath. She blew a steady flame onto the bottom of the pan. Sparks flew in all directions. There was a sizzling sound and a cloud of black smoke blew into the kitchen just as Gertrude took another deep breath. She jumped backwards coughing loudly and dropped the frying pan with a clatter onto the kitchen floor. The pancake lay on the tiles, a smoking, black lump.

"Overcooked it!" Gertrude spluttered crossly.

Upstairs, Meg barked noisily which woke first Nellie and Sam, and then Dad and Granny May. Lights went on all over the house as Meg rushed downstairs.

Gertrude looked at the mess she had made and realized it was time to go. She climbed onto the window sill and heaved and puffed and pushed. It was no good. She was fatter than when she came in. She was not going to get out through the window.

Gertrude heard footsteps coming down the stairs. Already Meg was sniffing at the charred pancake. Gertrude dived for the broom cupboard. She squeezed herself between the brushes and dusters and shut the door.

She was just in time. Dad came cautiously into the kitchen clutching a poker.

"Goodness gracious! What a mess!" he exclaimed. He saw the burnt frying pan and smoking pancake, the open refrigerator door and flour everywhere.

"It's all right," he called over his shoulder. "They've gone." Granny May came in carrying a shovel and Nellie came in holding Sam.

"Whoever was here got away through the window," said Dad.

"They've stolen all our food," said Granny May. "*And* ruined the frying pan into the bargain."

"Why didn't you bark sooner, Meg?" asked Dad. Meg looked hurt. After all it was only Gertrude and Gertrude did live in the shed.

Gertrude was Nellie's friend.

Nellie stood wide-eyed. She had noticed the end of something sticking out from under the broom cupboard door. She recognized it at once as the end of Gertrude's tail.

"I'm going to telephone the police," said Dad. "Don't touch anything in case the burglar left some finger prints." And off he went to dial 999.

"Come on, Nellie," Granny May said. "Back to bed."

Nellie could see Meg sniffing at the broom cupboard door. "Poor Gertrude," Nellie thought. "What shall I do?"

Granny May ushered Nellie and Meg into the hall. "Now go along," she said. "Upstairs at once and back to bed."

Nellie went upstairs but stopped on the first landing. She could hear Dad talking on the telephone in the front room. The receiver went down. There was silence for a bit before Granny May began to talk in a low voice.

Nellie tiptoed downstairs and along the hallway to the kitchen. She carefully opened the door and closed it behind her. She rushed to the broom cupboard and flung back the door. Gertrude was half hidden underneath the dusters trying to stifle an attack of hiccups.

"Quick," said Nellie. "Dad's rung the

police." Nellie unlocked the back door and pushed Gertrude towards it.

"It's all right, I'm going. There's no need to push," Gertrude said ungratefully.

"Hurry up," said Nellie.

"I know when I'm not wanted. I'm going," said Gertrude. She walked to the door and promptly got stuck trying to get through. "Give us a shove, Nellie."

"You've eaten too much," Nellie said. "You're plain greedy. You don't know when to stop."

"Hurry up and push before I'm arrested," Gertrude said trying to wriggle her way out. "Or I'll have to burn the door down."

"You wouldn't!" gasped Nellie.

"I might have to."

Nellie pushed and Gertrude shot out into the dark of the garden.

"I'll pop off for forty winks. Thank you, Nellie," she hiccupped from the dark. "Bring me a sack of charcoal for when I wake up, will you?"

"Yes, yes, all right. Now go!"

"Night, night," Gertrude called.

Forty winks for a dragon, as Nellie well knew, could last anything from a day to a week, which Nellie thought a good thing under the circumstances.

"What are you doing still up?" asked Granny May coming into the kitchen. "And who were you talking to?"

"The dragon," said Nellie. "She's gone off for forty winks."

"We'll have none of your imaginings just now, young lady. Up those stairs at once," said Granny May.

As Nellie went upstairs to bed the police arrived. "It's just as well they don't believe in dragons or Gertrude would really be in trouble," Nellie decided.

The policemen thought it a funny sort of burglar who ate everything and burnt frying pans. They set to work to find the burglar's fingerprints. But, of course, there weren't any. Meanwhile the burglar was asleep in the shed dreaming of pancakes.

7 Nellie Goes to the Zoo

Nellie was ready. She stood by the front door dressed in a red woolly pullover, yellow dungarees and her smart green shoes. She had pinned the dragon badge she had made to the front of her dungarees. It said "Dragon Power" all round the edge and in the middle Nellie had drawn a picture of Gertrude. She was wearing it today because Dad was taking her and Floyd to the zoo as a treat.

"No, Meg, you can't come," Nellie said as Meg dropped her lead on the front door mat and wagged her tail. "Dogs aren't allowed at the zoo." Meg's tail drooped and she went back to the kitchen and sat in her basket.

"Hurry up, Dad," Nellie called and opened the front door.

Floyd was waiting on the pavement. He had on his new trainers, a denim suit and a yellow and red cap with an F on the front.

"I like the badge," he said.

"I made it to please Gertrude," said Nellie.

"Oh, yes," said Floyd and changed the subject. He didn't want to hurt Nellie's feelings but he didn't believe in dragons and that was that.

"Do you think we'll be able to have a ride on an elephant?" he asked.

"We'll have to ask Dad," said Nellie.

They asked him as soon as he opened the door. He wasn't sure.

"You'll have to wait and see," he said.

They climbed into Nellie's dad's car. Granny May waved to them as they drove off. Nellie and Floyd waved through the back window.

It took ages getting to the zoo. Dad said it wasn't far but it seemed like forever. When they spotted a sign which said "To the Zoo" it began to get exciting. They kept looking. They both wanted to be the first to see it.

"There it is!" they said as Dad swung the car into the car park. They could see the tops of tall cages and some rocks which went up high behind a tall fence. They ran across the car park to the entrance. Dad caught them up and bought the tickets. They pushed through the turnstile and were, at last, in the zoo.

Dad wanted to know what they would like to look at first.

"I'd like to see the elephants," Floyd said.

"I want to see the monkeys," Nellie said.

"But which first?" asked Dad.

"Elephants," said Floyd.

"Monkeys," said Nellie.

In the end, Dad tossed a coin and Nellie called "Heads" and lost. They set off down a path where a signpost pointed "To the Elephant House". They were nearing the end of the path when something in the sky caught Nellie's eye. It looked awfully like the shape of a distant dragon. Nearer and nearer came the shape, and clearer and clearer it became.

"Come on, Nellie," said Floyd. "What are you staring at?"

"Oh, nothing," said Nellie, thinking to herself, "It's Gertrude. I hope she doesn't do anything naughty."

What Nellie didn't know was that when she and Floyd had been talking on the pavement waiting for Dad, Gertrude was on the roof having a doze against the chimney stack. She woke up in time to hear them talking about elephants. Elephants sounded exciting. She had followed the car. It couldn't have been easier. Gertrude landed on the Elephant House roof.

"I guessed," she said to herself, "that it was either the circus or the zoo they were going to. I was right."

Gertrude wondered what to look at. Below her was a large yard and in it were two elephants, a mother and a baby. Both were munching hay from a large pile the keeper had left for them.

"Ah, how sweet," said Gertrude. She spotted Nellie in the crowd behind the railways.

"Nellie," she called and waved an arm.

Nellie looked up. No one else noticed Gertrude as she did a little dance across the roof.

"She's showing off," thought Nellie. "I'm not going to take any notice." Gertrude didn't like being ignored and flew off in a huff.

Floyd liked the elephants. He loved the way their trunks curled around the hay and tucked it into their mouths. He liked the way they munched.

"I wish I could take the baby elephant home," he said. Dad laughed.

"I don't think your mum and dad would be very pleased if you did that," he said.

Leaving the elephants they followed the sign to the Monkey House. Nellie glanced quickly about her. Gertrude had disappeared. The monkey house was a large white building. They went in through the door and found lots of cages to walk around. Each cage had monkeys in. Some were small, others were large. In one cage at the end of the monkey house were two gorillas.

"Don't they look fierce?" said Nellie. But they weren't doing anything fierce. Just sitting and looking.

"It must be boring being in a cage all day," said Floyd.

"I like the chimpanzees," said Nellie. "Look, they're having fun." The two chimpanzees in the cage were playing chase. As soon as one caught the other it ran off and the other chased after it. Round and round the cage they raced, squealing with delight.

"There's nothing in the next cage," Floyd said. Nellie looked.

"Are you sure?" Nellie's eyes opened wide, for there, lying in the corner on a pile of straw was Gertrude, fast asleep. Or was she? Gertrude opened her eyes, winked and closed them again. "Oh, no!" gasped Nellie. "They've captured Gertrude."

Nellie wanted to set Gertrude free as quickly as possible. Leaving Floyd and Dad watching the chimpanzees she slipped away unnoticed and went through a door which said "No Entry Except Staff". She ran along a passageway. On either side were doorways.

"These must be the doors to the cages," Nellie thought. She stopped and counted the doors.

"This is the one. They've locked Gertrude in here," she said. Nellie drew back the bolts. She opened the door and looked in. She found herself face to face with a chimpanzee. Nellie tried to swing the door shut but the chimpanzee was too quick for her. It knocked her off balance and pushed her over. The other chimpanzee followed, grinning. The crowd stared, amongst them Dad and Floyd. They could hardly believe what they were seeing. Nellie had let out the chimpanzees.

"Nellie!" yelled Dad, at last. "What do you think you're doing?"

Nellie slammed the door shut and raced to the next cage. The door was unbolted. She opened it and looked inside. Gertrude had gone.

"Oh, no," she groaned. Nellie shut the door. "Dad's going to be really mad about this. Maybe if I capture the chimpanzees he'll forgive me."

How she was going to do this she had no idea. Nellie found a door which led outside. She looked around it. All was clear so she went outside. There was great activity outside the monkey house. Keepers were running in all directions with ropes and nets.

"Bananas," said Nellie. "If I could find some bananas I could tempt the chimps back to their cage."

"Psst!" hissed a voice. Nellie turned round.

"Over here," whispered the voice.

"Where?" asked Nellie.

"Here, behind the door, twit."

The door to the monkey house was slightly open. Nellie poked her head round it and saw Gertrude. "What are you doing?"

"Capturing the chimps, that's what," said Gertrude. She held up her front paws. In each one she held a hairy hand.

"I did it with bananas," she grinned. "I filled them up. It didn't take long. They're very greedy."

Gertrude led the two hiccupping chimpanzees back to their cage. Nellie opened the door. Gertrude led them in and let them go. Nellie locked the door. "Fancy a banana?" asked Gertrude. "I've found a place where there are masses."

"No thanks," said Nellie. "I'd better go and find Dad."

Nellie turned to go. "So you weren't captured then?" she asked.

"Who me? No, I was having a rest."

Dad and Floyd were outside looking for her. They were worried. "Where have you been?" Dad wanted to know.

"We thought you must have been eaten," said Floyd.

"I've been looking for the chimpanzees but it's all right. They're back in their cages. Gertrude found them and fed them bananas," said Nellie.

"How can you make up a story at a time like this," fumed Dad.

"Look, the chimps are back!" said Floyd. Dad looked.

"Well, that just about takes the biscuit," he said. Nellie shrugged. She was getting used to not being believed.

"We'd better go home before the keepers find Nellie and lock her up," said Floyd.

"They wouldn't, would they?" said Nellie.

"I don't think we should take any chances," said Dad. "They were very angry when the chimps were let out."

When they got to the car park Gertrude was sitting on top of the car washing her paws.

"I'm hitching a ride home," she told Nellie. "I've eaten too many bananas to fly."

Nellie didn't say anything. She was wishing she had asked Gertrude if she needed rescuing before rushing off and making a mistake. She looked glum.

"Cheer up," called down Gertrude. "It was a good adventure. The bananas were great."

"I suppose it was," said Nellie. "But we didn't see all of the zoo."

"Never mind, you can finish looking next time you come," said Gertrude. "You can never see all there is to see at once."

"I suppose you're right," Nellie said wondering what Granny May would have to say about it all when they got home.

8 Nellie and the Soggy Bonfire

Nellie pulled on her playing-in-the-garden dungarees. It was a sunny Sunday morning, so Dad and Granny May had decided to do the gardening. Nellie had decided to help. Meg woofed and chose her red ball from the toys in her basket. She always knew when Nellie was going into the garden — it meant fun.

"Woof, woof," barked Meg, dropping her ball and picking it up after every woof.

Nellie went to grab the ball but Meg was too quick for her. She picked it up and chewed it, growling at the same time.

"I don't want your soggy old ball. You can

keep it," said Nellie as she tied the laces of her trainers.

"Didn't you hear what I said?" Nellie asked.

Then, as quick as anything, she grabbed the ball and raced downstairs. Meg ran after her barking. Nellie charged into the kitchen and crashed into Dad. Meg slithered across the floor and crashed into them both.

"Nellie!" said Dad.

"Sorry," said Nellie and dashed into the garden. Meg scampered after her.

Once outside Nellie threw the ball down the garden as hard as she could. It sailed over the lawn, over the vegetable patch and landed in the wilderness.

"Go on, Meg. Fetch!" cried Nellie. Meg tore down the garden after the ball and disappeared amongst the brambles.

Dad came out of the back door and pulled on his wellingtons. He opened the outhouse door and fetched his gardening tools. He wheeled them down the garden in his wheelbarrow.

"I'm going to do weeding," he said. "If the weather stays fine we could have a barbeque later."

"I'll help," said Nellie. She was hoping that Dad wouldn't notice the missing sacks of charcoal that she had taken for Gertrude.

Nellie began to pull weeds from the flower bed at the side of the lawn. Meg came bounding down the garden wagging her tail like anything. She was in time to see Granny May take out the lawn mower. Meg had a "thing" about the lawn mower. At least that was what Nellie called it. Whenever anyone wanted to cut the grass Meg always got in the way by chasing the lawn mower.

Today was to be no different. As soon as she heard Granny May wheel the mower down the path she dropped her ball and ran at it growling, barking and snapping her teeth.

"Go away, Meg!" said Granny May. "I want to cut the grass without you interfering."

The lawn mower had a motor. It was started by pulling a long string. Granny May pulled the string and the motor spluttered into life. It roared as Granny May set off down one side of the lawn. Meg jumped at the lawn mower and barked and barked. Nellie put her hands over her ears. "What a row," she said, screwing up her face.

Someone, tucked up under the sacks in the old garden shed at the end of the garden, thought the same. It was Gertrude the dragon. She had been asleep for about a week and had been slowly waking up all morning when the dreadful row had started. She flung the sacks from her and climbed out of bed.

"That row is giving me a headache. If it's not one sort of row it's another! I can't stand it. It's got to stop," she said, flinging open the shed door and stomping into the garden. "A dragon has got to have a peaceful nap."

Gertrude flew onto the shed roof. She could just see over the brambles of the wilderness.

"Ah ha!" she said. "Grass cutting time. Right. We'll soon see about that."

Gertrude flew to the ground and picked up a handful of pebbles. She sneaked down the garden wall making sure that Nellie didn't see her and threw the pebbles across the lawn as Granny May mowed past her.

"That'll fix it," she said and sneaked back to bed closing the shed door behind her.

At the end of the lawn Granny May turned the mower and mowed towards the house. Meg barked savagely at the noisy green machine. Suddenly there was the sound of thudding and pinging as Granny May mowed over the pebbles. She stopped the mower at once. Meg stopped barking.

"Peace at last," sighed Gertrude under the sacks.

"Nellie," said Granny May. "Have you put stones on the grass?"

"No," said Nellie. "Of course I haven't."

"Somebody has. The grass is covered in them."

"It wasn't me, honestly," said Nellie.

"Come and help me pick them up," said Granny May.

As Nellie and Granny May picked up the pebbles Meg wandered off to fetch her ball. The earth where Nellie had been weeding was nice and soft so Meg put her ball on it and began to dig. Earth flew across the grass. Meg was enjoying herself. This was to be a really big hole, she decided.

"Stop that dog," Dad cried from the vegetable patch.

"No, Meg. Naughty dog," said Nellie.

Meg stopped digging and wondered what all the fuss was about.

"Clear off," said Dad charging at her with a spade.

Meg picked up her ball and ran into the wilderness leaving Nellie to fill up the hole and clear the earth from the lawn. Meg looked for somewhere else to dig. She put her ball down by the old shed and watched it roll slowly into a hole. She sniffed after it. The hole went under the shed. Meg wagged her tail. It thumped against the shed door. Scrabble, scrabble, scrabble went her front feet in the hole. Meg was having a lovely time!

Inside the shed under the sacks Gertrude began to hiss. She flung back the sacks. "A dragon is entitled to doze," she muttered. "A dragon is entitled to a little peace and quiet."

Gertrude listened to the thudding sound on the door and the scrabbling sound from under the floor. Her eyes glinted. "Meg," she said. "I'll fix her."

Gertrude pushed her claws down the side of a floor board and pulled. As the board lifted up she caught sight of Meg's head and the ball. Gertrude grabbed the ball and pushed the floor board back into place. She hopped outside. Meg came out of the hole in time to see Gertrude take a deep breath, throw the ball in the air and blow a stream of fire onto it. The ball became a red blob which splatted to the ground. Gertrude turned her nose in the air and stomped back into the shed, banging the door behind her.

Meg sniffed at the blob. It was hot. It should have been her ball but it wasn't. As the blob cooled Meg went closer. Very carefully she lifted the blob in her teeth. She took it back through the wilderness and dropped it at Nellie's feet. Nellie took one look.

"Gertrude," she said. She picked up the blob and set off for the shed. Meg trotted at her heels. Granny May started the lawn mower.

"Quick, Meg, follow me," said Nellie as Meg turned to bark. Meg did as she was told.

When they got to the shed the door burst open. Gertrude came out steaming. Smoke was pouring through her nostrils. As she spoke sparks flew from her mouth.

"I can't stand it any more," she said to Nellie. "A dragon has to have peace."

"I think you're an old meany-boots to melt

Meg's ball. What did you do that for?" Nellie asked.

"Noise. She was making a noise."

"Look," said Nellie. "It's Sunday morning. The garden has to be dug and the lawn mowed."

"But a dragon has to *doze* before it wakes up!"

"Have you thought of ear plugs?" asked Nellie.

"What are they?"

"You put them in your ears to stop the noise coming in. I can make you some, if you like, out of cotton wool."

"Would you, Nellie? Would you really?"

"Meg, we'll have to pretend your ball's a flying saucer," Nellie said. Meg wagged her tail.

"I won't melt any more balls if you make me some ear plugs," promised Gertrude. "And when I've had my doze, I'll come and help in the garden. I will, really I will."

Nellie ran indoors to fetch the cotton wool. When she got back to the shed Gertrude was all tucked up and waiting. Nellie stuffed loads of cotton wool into each ear. Soon Gertrude couldn't hear the lawn mower any more. She waved to Nellie and Meg as they went out. Her eyelids drooped and she dozed.

By the time they got back to the lawn Granny May had finished cutting the grass.

"What on earth's happened to Meg's ball?" she asked, looking at the red blob Meg was carrying.

"The dragon melted it," said Nellie. "It's a flying saucer now."

Granny May laughed. "You do tell some tall stories, Nellie. Come on, help me get the bonfire ready."

Nellie and Granny May gathered together all the garden rubbish they could find. Granny May fetched some newspapers and a box of matches. They scrunched the newspaper into balls and covered it carefully with the garden bits and pieces. Granny May lit the newspaper and soon the bonfire was blazing.

It was then the first spot of rain fell. Soon other spots came one after another.

"Oh, no!" cried Nellie. "The bonfire'll go out."

Dad collected his garden tools and Granny May wheeled in the lawn mower. The rain was falling fast. "Come in, Nellie, before you get soaked," called Granny May.

Nellie looked at the bonfire. The raindrops were hissing into the flames. Soon the bonfire would be out. Nellie watched from indoors. The rain poured down.

"I was going to make baked potatoes," she said.

"Never mind," said Granny May. "We'll do baked potatoes in the oven. They're almost as good."

The rain didn't last for long. "Well, I'm blowed," said Granny May. "The rain's stopped. It was just a heavy shower." The clouds looked less black and there was even a patch of blue sky. "Let's get the bonfire going, Nellie," said Granny May.

They fetched some more newspaper and went into the dripping garden. They scrunched the newspaper into balls and covered the balls with sticks. Granny May struck a match. The nespaper burnt but the wood didn't.

"It's too wet," said Nellie. "I knew it would be."

Meg barked and put her red blob at Nellie's feet. But Nellie wouldn't play. So Meg trotted down the garden to the wilderness to do more digging.

As she got to the shed, the door opened and Gertrude came out. She was properly awake at last. She did a long stretch and pulled out her ear plugs. Meg wagged her tail and dropped the red blob at Gertrude's feet. Gertrude picked it up and threw it. It sailed over the wilderness and the vegetable patch and landed in the middle of the bonfire surprising both Nellie and Granny May. Meg came charging after it.

Gertrude flew onto the wall. She watched as Nellie picked up the red blob which was covered in soggy ashes.

"Now who threw that?" Granny May asked.

"Gertrude, I expect," said Nellie.

"What nonsense!" said Granny May. "It was Floyd, I shouldn't wonder. I expect he's hiding."

Gertrude hopped along the wall. "It was me," she said. "I'm awake."

But Granny May didn't hear and didn't see Gertrude because she didn't believe in dragons. She took the red blob indoors to wash it.

"The rain spoiled the bonfire," said Nellie. "I was going to bake potatoes."

"Bake potatoes," said Gertrude who was always hungry when she woke up. "Yummy."

"But I can't because the bonfire won't light."

"I'll soon get it going," Gertrude said. "You go and fetch the potatoes."

Nellie ran indoors. Gertrude took a long deep breath and blew. A long flame hit the bonfire. It began to spit, crack and hiss. Gertrude took another deep breath and an-

other. The bonfire blazed. Gertrude flung more and more rubbish onto it. She blew and blew. The bonfire grew bigger and bigger.

When Nellie came back with the potatoes she was delighted.

"That's enough, Gertrude," Nellie said. "The potatoes will cook in that easily." But Gertrude wouldn't stop. She looked around the garden to see what else she could burn and spying Dad's beansticks in the vegetable patch pulled them up one by one. She threw them on the bonfire.

"Stop," cried Nellie. "Gertrude, stop."

Gertrude was hungry. "The bigger the bonfire the sooner I get my potatoes," she thought. Next she grabbed the garden table and that went into the flames. She began pulling at the pear tree.

"No, Gertrude, *no!*"

Nellie ran for the hose pipe as fast as she could. She fixed the end to the garden tap and turned it on. She grabbed the nozzle and ran with it to the bonfire. Water came gushing out. She hosed until the flames sizzled and died. She kept hosing. Soon the bonfire was out. Carefully, testing to see if it was hot, she pulled the garden table onto the lawn. It was a bit charred here and there but it was still a table. The beansticks had gone. Gertrude couldn't understand it.

"What did you do that for?" she asked.

"Trust you to go too far," said Nellie. "I'm going to get the blame for this." Which is, of course, exactly what happened. Gertrude stomped back to the garden shed muttering.

"I was only trying to be helpful."

When Dad saw that his beansticks had gone and the state of the table he really told Nellie off. Granny May made baked potatoes in the oven after all. Later, Nellie took some cold ones to the shed for Gertrude.

"I'm sorry," Gertrude said. "I did get a bit carried away."

She blew on the potatoes until they were steaming and munched.

9 Nellie and the Snowy Day

Nellie woke up and stretched. It was morning. She could see daylight through the crack in the curtains. Meg lay on the bed watching her. Nellie put her hand on Meg's head and stroked her ears. All of a bustle, Meg jumped off the bed and fetched her blue rubber bone. She jumped up beside Nellie and shook her head.

"I don't want to pull it," said Nellie. "It's too early."

Meg growled and shook her head again. She put the end of the bone in Nellie's hand. Nellie pulled. Meg pulled even harder. Soon the pillows were flying and the bedclothes were all

over the floor. Nellie shouted and Meg growled
ferociously. Granny May put her head round
the door.

"What a row," she said. "Do you have to?"

"Meg thinks she's winning but I am," said
Nellie holding up the blue bone. Meg jumped at
it and Nellie threw it in the air. Meg dug up a
pillow to find it.

"I think you should pull the curtains," said
Granny May. "You might have a nice
surprise."

"What surprise?" Nellie asked.

But Granny May only said, "Breakfast'll be
ready in ten minutes."

Nellie bounced across her bed and pulled
back the curtains. Outside the world was
covered in white. "It's snowed!" she cried. "It's
snowed in the night, Meg."

Nellie ran to the bathroom and had the

quickest wash in the world. She scrubbed her teeth until the toothpaste flew. She dashed back to her bedroom and pulled on her clothes.

"It's snowed," she cried. "And it's Saturday. We can play and play all day!"

Meg was excited too and shook her bone vigorously.

After breakfast Nellie pulled on her thick, red, woolly jumper with the green frog on the front.

"My Ferdi Frog jumper'll keep me really warm," she said. Two pairs of socks were pulled onto her feet. Mittens were found and her warm jacket with the furry hood. At last, Nellie pulled on her wellington boots. She was ready.

"I'm going to see if Floyd wants to come to the park," she said. Floyd did want to come. He was tucked up nice and warm and carried a tin tray under his arm.

"What's the tray for?" Nellie asked. They set off down the road with Meg at their heels.

"It's for tobogganing," said Floyd. "My mum told me how she used to toboggan on a tray and she gave me this old tin one."

"Great," said Nellie. "Just great."

They crunched through the snow as fast as they could. It was slippery and they clung to each other to stop themselves from falling over.

"Meg's all right," said Nellie. "She doesn't seem to slip at all."

"That's because she's got four legs instead of two," said Floyd.

When they got to the park the gates were open and the park keeper was clearing snow from the path. He looked cross and fed up. The children hurried past him. "Remember to keep that dog from digging in the flower beds," he said when he saw Meg.

"I will," said Nellie wondering if she would know where the flower beds were under the snow.

"Doesn't it look nice?" said Floyd gazing through the trees at the snow on the other side.

"Yes," said Nellie. "It looks wonderful."

They left the path and ran into the snow. Meg leapt after them. They picked up handfuls of crispy whiteness and threw snowballs at one another. Meg tried to catch them in her teeth.

"Look at Meg," said Nellie. "She's turning into a snowball herself."

Meg's fur had collected lots of snow. There were great lumps glued to her coat where the fur was long. She didn't seem to mind and began to dig a snow hole.

"Let's toboggan," said Floyd. It took a moment or two to find the tray and they were off, running towards the hill. At the top Floyd put down the tray and sat on it.

"Ready?" shouted Nellie.

"Ready!" said Floyd, holding the sides. Nellie gave him a push. Floyd began to move down the hill going faster and faster. He yelled with delight. By the time he got to the bottom he could hold on no longer. The tray went one way and he went the other, rolling over and over until he came to a stop. He flung his arms in the air and shouted, "Fantastic!"

He picked up the tray and began to climb up the hill. Nellie was waiting at the top looking forward to her go.

"That looks fun," said a voice behind her.

Nellie turned round and found Gertrude. "Can I have a go?" asked the dragon.

"Don't be silly," said Nellie. "You're much too big. Your bottom wouldn't fit on the tray."

"What do you mean?" said Gertrude stiffly. "Are you saying that my bottom is fat?"

"No, I'm not," said Nellie. "But it *is* bigger than Floyd's or mine."

"I see," said Gertrude. She turned away.

"Where are you going?"

"To get on with my keep fit. I can take a hint. You think I'm too fat."

"I didn't say anything of the sort," Nellie said.

"You didn't say it in so many words but you said it," replied Gertrude. Her nose went into the air and she marched off.

"Who were you talking to?" Floyd asked when he arrived at the top.

"To Gertrude," said Nellie.

"Oh, come on, Nellie. Why do you keep on with that stuff about a dragon when you know I don't believe it?"

"Just because you don't believe it doesn't mean she doesn't exist," Nellie said and got on the tray.

Floyd gave her a push. She slid down the hill. Gertrude watched from behind a tree.

"It's so bumpy," Nellie cried. "I can't stay on." Nellie, like Floyd, ended up in a heap in the snow. This was Gertrude's chance. She flew

from her hiding place down the hill. With a graceful swoop she picked up the tin tray and glided off with it. It was gone before Nellie got to her feet.

"Where did the tray go?" Nellie asked.

Floyd came slithering down the hill to help look. Nellie didn't notice Gertrude at the top of the hill wriggling her bottom onto the tray. She could only get half of it on at once.

"Oh, botheroo!" she said. "It *is* too small." She pushed forward. "Here I go!"

Meg barked encouragement. Nellie looked up. "So that's where it's gone," she said. "That dratted dragon."

"What do you mean?" Floyd asked looking but not seeing anything. Not even the edge of the tray because Gertrude covered it so completely.

"Gertrude's pinched the tray."

"You're a nutcase," said Floyd not knowing what else to say. After all the tray had disappeared.

"Watch out," said Nellie pushing Floyd out of the way and landing in a heap on top of him.

"Nellie," he shouted. "Why did you have to do that?"

"She tried to run us over," said Nellie clambering up.

Gertrude came to a bumpy halt. "It's great," she shouted. "I'm going to do it again."

"You've bent the tray," shouted Nellie.

"Not very much," said Gertrude and flew back up the hill.

"What do you mean, 'you've bent the tray'? Where *is* the tray?" Floyd asked.

"Watch out," Nellie said pushing Floyd out of the way again.

"That's not funny," Floyd said. He was getting fed up. He wanted his tray back.

"Give it back, Gertrude," said Nellie.

"You can have it," said Gertrude. She threw the tray across the snow and it landed near Floyd.

"I've found it," Floyd cried. He picked it up. They looked at it. It was bent and buckled to the shape of half Gertrude's bottom. Neither of them would be able to sit on it now.

"How did that happen?" Floyd said. "You must have hit a bump."

Nellie didn't say anything. She was so cross. She could see Gertrude doing her exercises on the top of the hill. She hoped she would stay away from them for the rest of the morning.

"Let's make a snowman," she suggested. "It can have the tray for a hat. It's almost the right shape."

Floyd liked the idea and the two of them began rolling a giant snowball for the body. As soon as they began their snowman they noticed other children doing the same.

"Our park is going to have lots of snow-men," Nellie said.

"We could make them in a big circle," Floyd suggested.

"That's a good idea," Nellie agreed.

Floyd went and asked the other children if they would like to make a circle of snowmen. Some of them thought they would. Soon five snowmen were being built facing into a circle. The children patted and moulded the snow into arms and heads. They made buttons and eyes from stones they found in the snow holes Meg had dug. Pieces of twig made mouths and noses.

Nellie and Floyd put the tin tray on the head of their snowman. One had a scarf around his neck, another a pom pom hat on his head. They looked fine. The children were pleased. They left the snowmen and wandered off to play hide and seek.

Gertrude was doing running exercises. She saw the snowmen from the top of the hill. She trotted and slithered down to them, puffing, her hot breath making clouds of steam.

"What on earth are they? Sort of snow people." She did running on the spot. "I could do my deep breathing exercises with these," she said. "After all, they can't want them any more."

She stood in the middle of the circle and took a deep breath in through her nostrils and out again. Jets of steam blew around one of the snowmen. It began to melt. Gertrude turned to the next snowmen and blew. Then the next and the next. Soon all the snowmen were running with water.

Nellie discovered her. She beat her fists against Gertrude's scaly body.

"You beast, you beast, you've melted our snowmen," she cried.

Gertrude wriggled and pushed Nellie away. "Oh, don't," she said. "That tickles."

"How *could* you?" Nellie said.

"I thought you had finished with them."

"There's no snow left to make any more!" Nellie cried.

Gertrude looked about her. There was a criss cross of green lines where the giant snowballs had been rolled. Nearly all the snow had gone showing the grass underneath.

"Sorry," she said. "I'll mend them for you really I will."

"Where will you find any snow?"

"Leave that to me," said Gertrude. "I'm going to get a lot more exercise. Goody, goody."

She flew into the air with a great flapping of wings. She went very high and landed on top of a snow covered tree. She jumped from branch to branch pushing and pulling and shaking. Snow cascaded to the ground.

Nellie cheered up at once. She rushed to the bottom of the tree and carried armful after armful of fresh snow to the circle of snowmen. Gertrude arrived panting.

"I'll help," she said.

By the time Floyd came over, all the snowmen were looking as good as new. "I think it's time to go home," he said. "My hands and feet are freezing. We can come and see our snowmen tomorrow."

Gertrude, who was feeling in a good mood,

nearly blew hot air at Floyd but remembered in time not to. She didn't want to do any more melting.

When they got home Nellie said goodbye to Floyd on the front doorstep.

"It was a great morning," he said.

"It was," Nellie agreed.

Nellie and Meg went through their house to the kitchen. Making sure that Granny May wasn't watching, Nellie took a whole packet of chocolate biscuits from the biscuit tin. She and Meg took it to the old garden shed.

"This is for you," she said to Gertrude who was lying across her pile of sacks resting.

"Thank you, Nellie," Gertrude said. "No hard feelings?" Nellie grinned and shook her head. They left Gertrude munching the biscuits. The pair of them ran down the garden and back into the warmth of the house.

10 Nellie Goes to the Park

Nellie pulled on her red mackintosh and checked in her bag to see if she had remembered everything. Meg's blue ball, bread for the ducks, the jam jar with string around the top, her peanut butter sandwiches for elevenses and a handkerchief. Granny May always said to take a handkerchief just in case. Yes, that was everything.

Meg bounded off to fetch her lead. She guessed they were going to the park. Meg dropped the lead at Nellie's feet and barked. "Hurry up," her bark said. "Hurry up and let's get going!"

"I'm coming!" said Nellie. She pulled her bag over her shoulder, clipped Meg's lead to her collar and picked up her fishing net.

"Wait for me," said Granny May picking up her shopping bag.

Nellie, Granny May and Meg walked by Floyd's house. They saw Floyd looking glumly out of the window. Nellie waved. It was a shame Floyd couldn't come too but he had a cold. His dad said he had to stay indoors until it was better.

Meg trotted eagerly beside Nellie. When they reached the end of the street they turned left. The park entrance was a little way along the main road. "Nearly there," said Nellie.

The park gates were wide open. Nellie and Meg ran through them. Once in the park Nellie unclipped Meg's lead and threw the ball. Meg caught it and dashed off to play her own special game of hide and seek.

Granny May went with Nellie to find the park keeper. Nellie thought he was a grumpy, old man.

"Oh, it's *you*," he said when he saw them.

"Keep an eye on her for me," said Granny May, "I'm going to do some shopping."

"I will," said the park keeper.

"See you later, Nellie," said Granny May.

"Don't get up to any mischief." And off she went.

"Just you keep that dog off the flower beds," said the park keeper. "I don't want it digging up my tulips."

"I will," said Nellie with her sweetest smile. But when the park keeper turned his back she poked her tongue out at him.

Nellie's first thought was to get to the lake and feed the ducks. Nellie knew they would be on the island in the middle of the lake sitting under the silver birch trees.

"Come on, ducks," she called. She rustled the paper bag. The ducks splashed into the water and paddled over. They quacked with pleasure at the thought of getting something to eat. Nellie broke the bread into bits and threw it into the water. The ducks gobbled and squabbled until it was all gone, after which they slowly bobbed away. Nellie screwed up the paper bag and put it in the litter bin.

Next, she was going to go fishing. She took the jam jar from her bag and filled it with water. She picked up her net and was about to look for tiddlers when Meg arrived. Meg went to the water's edge, wagging her tail like anything and dropped the blue ball into it. It was a solid rubber ball, especially for dogs. It sank straight to the bottom. Meg looked at

Nellie as if to say, "Go on! Get it out."

"Very funny, Meg," said Nellie. She rolled up her sleeve and fished under the water with her hand. The water became brown and murky. Nellie pulled out the dripping ball and threw it across the grass. Meg was after it like lightning. Nellie shook her dripping arm and pulled down her sleeve. She peered into the murky water. She moved along the bank until the water became clearer. At last she spotted some minnows darting in and out of the weed.

Nellie lifted her net. Taking great care to go slowly she slid it into the water. She got quite close to the minnows when suddenly there was a great splash. "What was that?" said Nellie.

The minnows, frightened, disappeared. Nellie could see waves moving away from where the splash had been. Fat bubbles were popping to the surface in a long line that was making its way towards Nellie. Nellie gathered up her bits and pieces and moved quickly up the bank.

A head emerged from the water followed by a long neck and a gold and green body. It was Gertrude. She stood dripping; water up to her knees.

"Morning, Nellie," she said. "Did you see me dive in?"

"No, I didn't. You've just given me a

horrible fright."

"Me?" said Gertrude. "Harmless little old me?"

"Yes, *you*," said Nellie. "Harmless little old you."

"Well, if you're going to be like that, I'm off. I'm doing my keep fit, you know."

With a backward flip, Gertrude plunged into the lake and was gone. Nellie looked into the water. It was filthy. Fishing was impossible until Gertrude stopped churning up the mud. Nellie called Meg. She ran to Nellie and dropped the ball. She panted expectantly.

"So, you want to play?" Nellie asked. Meg wagged her tail. Nellie picked up the ball. Meg danced around her. Nellie threw the ball into the air. It bounced on a park bench and whizzed back across the path. It landed with a splash in the lake.

"Oh, no," Nellie said. Meg rushed to the water's edge and jumped in. With a yelp of surprise she jumped out again. Nellie put her hand in the water. It was hot. Steam was beginning to rise from it. A trail of bubbles spread across the middle of the lake.

"Oh, dear," said Nellie.

The ducks were stranded on the island. They quacked loudly. The lake had never been hot before. Gertrude's breath was turning the lake into a steam bath. "Poor fish," said Nellie. "They must be roasting hot."

Gertrude's head rose to the surface for a breath.

"Gertrude," Nellie called. "Please, will you come here!"

Gertrude obligingly flopped on her back and swam back stroke across the lake.

"Haven't you done enough keep fit for today?" Nellie asked.

Gertrude shook her head. Her foot trod on something hard. "What's this?"

It was Meg's blue ball. Meg barked.

"Yours is it?" Gertrude said and threw it across the grass. It landed in the litter bin. Meg ran to the bin and barked at it.

"You're making the water hot," Nellie said.

"What's wrong with that?"

"It's too hot for the fish and the ducks," Nellie said.

"I see. I see. You're saying I can't swim any more, is that it?"

"It would be better if you didn't swim," Nellie said.

"But I like swimming."

"Running's good for keeping fit," Nellie said helpfully.

Gertrude put her nose in the air. "I don't like running. It's undragonlike." She climbed out of the water and walked to the litter bin. She took a deep breath and blew into it. A long flame licked round the scraps of paper and set them alight.

"What did you do that for?" Nellie asked running for her jam jar.

"Because I felt like it."

Nellie sploshed water over the flames. She ran for more but the flames fizzled out. Meg's ball lay in the bottom of the basket, black. Nellie fished it out and washed it in the lake.

"It's not quite the same as it was but I think it'll be all right."

Meg took it in her mouth. It seemed fine to her.

Nellie looked to see where Gertrude had

gone. She was standing in the middle of the tulip bed picking the flowers and eating them one by one.

"Gertrude, stop it at once," Nellie cried.

"But they're delicious, simply delicious," munched Gertrude. "Keeping fit gives you an appetite, you know."

Nellie looked for the park keeper. "Please, stop," she begged.

Gertrude wouldn't. She munched one tulip after another.

"Quick, Meg. Let's go," Nellie said.

She collected her things and clipped Meg's lead to her collar. They were half way to the gate when they heard the park keeper bellow. Nellie looked back and saw him throw his hat to the ground and wave his arms with fury. They hurried on.

"Have you had enough already?" Granny May asked when they bumped into her at the gate. "Have you behaved yourselves?"

"We have but that dragon hasn't."

"Oh, Nellie, you and your make believe. You're always dreaming about dragons," Granny May said.

Nellie looked over her shoulder and saw Gertrude sitting in the tulip bed licking her claws.

"Come on," Nellie said. "Let's go home."

When they got to their street Nellie stopped at Floyd's house and took her elevenses in to share with him. As they munched the peanut butter sandwiches Nellie told Floyd what had happened in the park.

"It's a good story," Floyd said when Nellie

had finished. "It's a pity that dragons don't really exist. I wouldn't mind meeting one."

"Sometimes I wish they didn't," Nellie said. "But I'm glad they do!"

SHEPHERD'S PIE

Dorothy Clark

ISBN 0 590 70310 2   70p

"Jack the giant's mother was an excellent cook and she believed in using natural ingredients. So cottage pies had to have *real* cottages in them — with the result that for miles around there was not a cottage left standing."

The Woolly family were particularly worried. Their cottage had been taken by Jack's mother, and that was bad enough, but they could see there might be more trouble ahead. Mr Woolly was a shepherd. What if the giants decided to try shepherd's pie?

In the face of such danger, Sandy and Polly Wolly knew that they must take drastic action. What they did makes a most satisfying conclusion to this very funny story.

HARRIET AND THE CROCODILES

Martin Waddell

ISBN 0 590 703099   £1.00

Harriet spells trouble, for teachers and for everyone else, too. She is very upset when her pet yellow snail disappears but looks forward to selecting a new pet during the class trip to the zoo.

Why is it that only Harriet thinks her crocodile is sweet and charming?
An hilarious story introducing Harriet who is already a firm favourite with 7-9 year olds.

HARRIET AND THE HAUNTED SCHOOL

Martin Waddell

ISBN 0 590 70441 9   £1.25

Finding a horse for Anthea to practise sitting on wasn't much of a problem for Harriet. But choosing a place to keep it was! The Games Cupboard provided a cosy home and the horse could take it's excercise at night!

But the late-night ghostly hoofbeats terrified the cleaning lady, Ethel Bunch. There was only one solution: the Slow Street Vigilantes and the Anti-Hàrriet League had to join forces — and set up a phantom trap!

Harriet is back!

Other Hippo Books You Will Enjoy:

SHEPHERD'S PIE

Dorothy Clark

ISBN 0 590 70310 2   70p

"Jack the giant's mother was an excellent cook and she believed in using natural ingredients. So cottage pies had to have *real* cottages in them — with the result that for miles around there was not a cottage left standing."

The Woolly family were particularly worried. Their cottage had been taken by Jack's mother, and that was bad enough, but they could see there might be more trouble ahead. Mr Woolly was a shepherd. What if the giants decided to try shepherd's pie?

In the face of such danger, Sandy and Polly Wolly knew that they must take drastic action. What they did makes a most satisfying conclusion to this very funny story.

HARRIET AND THE CROCODILES

Martin Waddell

ISBN 0 590 703099   £1.00

Harriet spells trouble, for teachers and for everyone else, too. She is very upset when her pet yellow snail disappears but looks forward to selecting a new pet during the class trip to the zoo.

Why is it that only Harriet thinks her crocodile is sweet and charming?
An hilarious story introducing Harriet who is already a firm favourite with 7-9 year olds.

HARRIET AND THE HAUNTED SCHOOL

Martin Waddell

ISBN 0 590 70441 9   £1.25

Finding a horse for Anthea to practise sitting on wasn't much of a problem for Harriet. But choosing a place to keep it was! The Games Cupboard provided a cosy home and the horse could take it's excercise at night!

But the late-night ghostly hoofbeats terrified the cleaning lady, Ethel Bunch. There was only one solution: the Slow Street Vigilantes and the Anti-Harriet League had to join forces — and set up a phantom trap!

Harriet is back!